Badger's Bad Mood

To Max - H.O.

First published in hardback in Great Britain by Andersen Press in 1997.
First published in Picture Lions in 1999.

5 7 9 10 8 6 4

ISBN 0 00 664680-8

Picture Lions is an imprint of the Children's Division, part of HarperCollins Publishers Ltd,
77-85 Fulham Palace Road, Hammersmith, London W6 8JB

Text copyright © Hiawyn Oram 1997.
Illustrations copyright © Susan Varley 1997.

Printed and bound in Singapore by Imago. •

Badger's Bad Mood

Hiawyn Oram & Susan Varley

PictureLions

An Imprint of HarperCollinsPublishers

Bat had been to deliver Badger's post and now he brought news:
Badger was in a bad mood.

"But Badger's *never* in a bad mood," said Fieldmouse.

"He is now," said Bat. "He just sits there, staring. Speak to him –
he almost snaps your head off."

"I'll go and see him," said Mole.

"I'll go with you," said Squirrel.

So Mole, Squirrel and Rabbit went to see Badger.

He was sitting in his chair, in the gloom, his face like a dark cloud.

"Now, now, Badger," fussed Squirrel, "this won't do at all."
She switched on a light.

"Turn that off!" snapped Badger. "And leave me be."

Squirrel and Rabbit were most offended. They scurried away, tutting to themselves.

Mole hung around in the shadows. He felt very sad. Without Badger in a good mood *everything* seemed wrong. He rattled some cups, cleared his throat and opened and closed a cupboard.

"You still there, Mole?"

"Yes, yes. I'm still here!"

Badger heaved round in his chair. "I'm sorry about this. 'Spect I'll get over it. But right now, I'm all out of it, you know. *All out of it.*"

"Don't worry," said Mole worriedly. "We'll just wait."

But waiting for Badger to get over his bad mood wasn't that easy. The animals were very impatient.

"He was going to help me choose a holiday," said Bat, waving his holiday brochures.

"Perhaps we should get him a tonic," said Rabbit.

"And some puzzles to take his mind off things," said Squirrel.

"Well, take him something," said Rat. "We're supposed to be going fishing today!"

"I've a doctor friend staying," said Stoat. "I'll take her round. She'll soon put him right."

Badger, however, was having none of it.

"Close the curtains," he begged Mole. "Keep them away."

Mole stood guard at the door. "I'm sorry, but he's not seeing anyone."

"Well, we can't wait for ever," said Frog. "Make him see reason, Molie."

"Snap him out of it," said Weasel.

"I'll see what I can do," said Mole.

When they had all gone away, Mole watched Badger staring and dozing and turning heavily in his chair.

He remembered his words. *All out of it.*

Then he crept over to Badger's desk and very quietly borrowed some paper and pens and pencils.

The next morning a poster appeared, pinned to a tree in the clearing.

AWARDS CEREMONY

Tomorrow night in this clearing
awards will be presented
for everything.
Presenter:
Stoat's Friend the Doctor
Master of Ceremonies:
MOLE

Afterwards there'll be
juice and cakes,
music and dancing.

Dress:
Your best.

Everyone got very excited.

"I'm bound to win the Fairy Cake Award," said Squirrel.

"Maybe I'll win the Slow Dancing," said Miss Snail.

They spent the rest of the day wondering who was going to win what for what and working on what they were going to wear.

Meanwhile, Mole went to see Badger.

"You'll have to come, of course. A little bird tells me you may be getting something."

Badger's eyes moved sharply for the first time in days.

"Really?" His voice had some edge to it for the first time in days.

"S'pose my tuxedo needs a press. You wouldn't help me with that, would you, Mole?"

Mole helped Badger press his suit and waistcoat.

Then he ran home to press his own – not to mention prepare some speeches, write out certificates, order the juice and cakes, book the musicians and set up the clearing!

"Whose idea was this anyway?" he kept saying to himself. "I'll *never* be ready!"

But somehow, by the time everyone started arriving for the ceremony, he was ready.

He showed Stoat's doctor friend to the platform.

Then, out of the corner of his eye, he saw Badger slipping in at the back. "Well, that's a relief," he sighed.

"Excuse me?" said the doctor.

"Nothing," said Mole. "Let's begin."

The first award did go to Squirrel for Fairy Cakes and Miss Snail did win for Slow Dancing.

Frog won for Best Hopping and Most Gallant Courting.

Stoat won for Swimming, Weasel for Wiliness, Fieldmouse for Scurrying, Hedgehog for Eating The Most Crisps At One Sitting, Rat for Reading, Rabbit for First Aid and Bat for Most Musical Accordion Playing.

"And now," announced Mole. "We come to the last section."
He cleared his throat. "The award for Always Knowing The Best Way
Through The Woods … goes to …" There was an expectant hush.
   "Badger!"
The clapping and cheering were deafening.
When it had died down, Mole cleared his throat again.

"And to save yourself a trip back to your seat ... the award for Always Knowing What To Do In A Crisis ... *Badger!*"

Mole waited for the applause to fade. "And ... the award for Always Being There For Others ... *Badger!*
The award for Most Needed And Depended On ... *Badger!*
And finally ... the award for Most Loved Whatever His Mood ... *BADGER!*"

Badger blushed and bowed and bowed and blushed and fumbled with all his certificates.

"Oh my, oh my," he whispered to Mole. "This is too much!"

"No more than you deserve," said Mole over the scraping of chairs as everyone stood up to shout *Bravo*.

"And now tell me," said Badger taking Mole aside for a moment after the ceremony, "whose idea was all this?"

Mole blinked slowly. "Um … uh … I …"

"Well," said Badger, "whoever it was deserves a medal. Because, y'know, now and again, everyone needs to hear …"

"How much they're loved?" said Mole.

"And *appreciated*," bowed Badger.

"You said it," sighed Mole giving Badger a hug and stepping on to the dance floor to announce …

"*OK, Badger's back! Let's Boogie!*"